CAMP CHAOS!

CAMP CHAOS!

BY RICHARD ASHLEY HAMILTON

RANDOM HOUSE NEW YORK

Manufactured under licence granted to AMEET Sp. z o.o. by the LEGO Group.

AMEET Sp. z o.o.
Nowe Sady 6, 94–102 Łódź—Poland
ameet@ameet.eu
www.ameet.eu

www.LEGO.com

Published in the United States by Random House Children's Books, a division of Penguin Random House LLC, 1745 Broadway, New York, NY 10019, and in Canada by Penguin Random House Canada Limited, Toronto. Random House and the colophon are registered trademarks of Penguin Random House LLC.

rhcbooks.com

Educators and librarians, for a variety of teaching tools, visit us at RHTeachersLibrarians.com

ISBN 978-0-593-56881-1 (trade) — ISBN 978-0-593-56883-5 (ebook)

Printed in the United States of America
10 9 8 7 6 5 4 3 2 1

First Edition 2022

CONTENTS

CHARACTER PROFILES:

OWEN GRADY

Owen Grady is an animal behaviorist who is fascinated by dinosaurs. He is Jurassic World's *Velociraptor* trainer and a survival expert.

RED

Red is Owen's dog. A very loyal four-legged friend, Red usually stays by Owen's side. He always wants to help and takes very good care of Owen.

DARIUS BOWMAN

An excellent gamer and a dinosaur expert, Darius won his spot at Camp Cretaceous by completing a Jurassic World video game.

Brooklynn

Brooklynn is a teenage social media superstar who's never parted from her smartphone. Being an extremely popular influencer and vlogger, she was brought into the park to post about her adventures and attract new campers.

Kenji Kon

A laid-back, quite lazy, and rather selfish son of a wealthy Jurassic World park investor. Kenji's full of himself, regularly trying to impress those around him, which often leads to trouble.

Yasmina "Yaz" Fadoula

Yaz is a top track athlete sponsored by Jurassic World park. Not a very social person, Yaz prefers to sit alone and draw when she's not training.

BEN PINCUS

Ben is the timid, bookish son of a Jurassic World park employee. He has a lot of phobias, and his mom thought getting Ben a free pass to the camp would help him conquer these fears.

SAMMY GUTIERREZ

She is an outgoing, friendly camper whose family owns the ranch that provides the dinosaurs with beef. Sammy is very enthusiastic about being at Camp Cretaceous, perhaps a little too enthusiastic.

CLAIRE DEARING

As Assistant Park Operations Manager, Claire loves making sure the park functions properly and guests are satisfied with their visit.

THE ACU

The Asset Containment Unit guards make sure that the dinosaurs stay where they are supposed to be and the Jurassic World visitors are safe.

VIC HOSKINS

He is the Security Director at Jurassic World. Vic heads up the Asset Containment Unit. He thinks there's no problem that can't be solved with blunt force or a tranquilizer dart.

CHAPTER 1
HIGH STAKES

ROOOAAARRR!

The cry echoed across Isla Nublar and scared a flock of toucans. The birds were used to hearing roars. They lived on the same island as the dinosaurs of Jurassic World, after all. But on the jungle floor, a fabric trap held a *different* wild animal. It roared, lashed, and crashed—until the fabric was unzipped from the inside. Owen Grady stormed out and gasped for fresh air.

"How can it be this hard to build a tent?!" he yelled.

Normally, Owen considered himself calm under pressure. Then again, there was nothing "normal" about Jurassic World. Owen had learned that lesson once he started working at the theme park. But, as he looked at the thick booklet of instructions that came with the tent, his blood boiled. A diagram on the cover showed a pair of happy workers assembling the tent together—not one furious worker at his wit's end.

Of course, Owen thought. *This is a two-person job. If only I had some help . . .*

He turned and found a few toucans staring at him—plus six teens named Darius, Brooklynn, Kenji, Yasmina, Ben, and Sammy. These kids came from different

parts of the world, but they all had two things in common. One, they were the first members of Jurassic World's Camp Cretaceous program for young dino-fans. And two, every single one of them looked bored out of their mind. In the most cheerful voice he could manage, Owen said, "Okay, campers! Who wants to pitch in by pitching these tents with me?"

The kids' regular counselors, Dave and Roxie, were at a training retreat on the next island over, Isla Sorna. That was why Claire Dearing, one of Jurassic World's top managers, had volunteered Owen to act as a substitute camp counselor.

"There's nobody better to teach these campers how to, y'know, actually camp!" Claire had told Owen earlier. "All they've seen so far is the inside of the cushy Camp Cretaceous tree house. A few days roughing it with you is just what they need. Besides, you train raptors all day long. How hard can it be to wrangle a few teens?"

Maybe Claire's right, Owen thought. *I've trained Blue, Charlie, Delta, and Echo to follow my commands. Teaching these teenagers a thing or two about the great outdoors should be a piece of cake!*

Owen strolled up to Darius, the one camper who probably knew as much about dinosaurs as Owen. The boy was kneeling by some *Compsognathus* tracks that he had just found in the mud. The discovery had made Darius go from bored to giddy in a matter of seconds.

"Whatcha got there, Darius?" said Owen. "*Compy* tracks?"

"You know it!" Darius replied, excited. "And the only thing more awesome than finding these tracks is discussing 'em with a fellow *Compsognathus* fan!"

"I wouldn't say I'm a fan necessarily," Owen said. "*Compys* are fine, but—"

"Fun fact!" Darius blurted. "*Compys* are some of the fastest non-avian dinosaurs on record!"

"That's great," Owen said, with far less enthusiasm than Darius. "And it would also be great if you could help me build those tents just as fast—"

"Fun fact: An adult *Compsognathus* can grow to the size of a turkey!" Darius said, cutting off Owen again. "Isn't that wild?!"

"Uh, yeah . . . wild," Owen said, slowly backing away from Darius. "You know what? I think I'll find someone a little less, um . . . animated."

Owen moved on to Brooklynn, who was holding her cell phone camera at arm's length. She flipped her pink hair and said, "What up, Brooklanders! Are you ready for my fiercest vlog yet?"

Owen ducked as Brooklynn swung her arm around and recorded a video of his dog,

Red. The friendly mutt bit at a fly buzzing by but missed it.

"Adorbs!" Brooklynn squealed into her cell. "For more of Red's silly pet tricks, stay glued to my vlog! And don't forget to subscribe and comment below!"

Owen had a few choice comments of his own but kept them to himself. He then found Kenji, who was sprawled on a log like a lazy teenager on his couch.

"Wassup, Kenji Kon!" Owen said. He held out his hand for a high five . . . but it never came.

"How about you lend me a hand with those tents?" Owen said. "Then we can chillax and—"

"Yeah, I'm not really into the whole 'building' thing," Kenji interrupted. "Not since my dad forced me to work summers at his condo construction company. *Glamping's* more my thing. That's where you *pay* someone to make your yurt, Otis."

"It's Owen," Owen said between gritted teeth. "Not Otis."

Kenji lowered his sunglasses over his eyes and went back to napping.

Owen forced a smile and approached Yasmina. She ran in place, dropped to the ground, did a push-up, and repeated the routine over again.

"Yasmina, would you please—" Owen began.

"Can't. Training. Sorry," Yasmina grunted between up-downs.

Owen's shoulders slumped. He saw Ben standing off on his own. But before Owen could ask anything, Ben said, "I'm really sorry, Mr. Grady, but my mom says I'm allergic to the synthetic fabric in those tents. It gives me a rash."

Owen stomped away from Ben and reached his last hope, Sammy.

"How's it goin', Owen?" Sammy said, beaming. "Ha ha, I love to rhyme! And I'd love to help with those rascally tents! Back on my family farm, we use pup tents, but those always make me think of those pastry thingies you put in your toaster, and then they pop up and they taste all warm and gooey and—"

"Okay, okay, you're hired!" Owen said, interrupting her. "Just keep the chitchat to a minimum. I've already got a headache from tango-ing with those tents in this heat. . . ."

Sammy mimed zipping her lips and followed Owen back toward the bundle of fabric and poles he'd just barely escaped. And, with Sammy no longer talking a mile a minute, Owen's headache started to fade. He wanted to keep the quiet going, so Owen pointed to a hammer and drew an imaginary line from the head of the hammer to the top of the tent stake in his hand. His meaning

was clear—drive the stake into the ground by whacking it with the hammer. Sammy nodded in understanding and swung down with the hammer.

But, instead of striking the stake, the hammer accidentally hit Owen's hand, causing him to cry out in pain. The stake went flying across the grass and landed beside one of the watching toucans. The bird grabbed it and flew away with her new toy as Owen let out one final frustrated roar.

CHAPTER 2
STARS AND YIPES

Across Isla Nublar, Jurassic World ran like clockwork. Thousands of tourists entered the famous theme park. They oohed and aahed at the futuristic buildings, thrilling rides, and main attractions—real live dinosaurs!

It was Claire Dearing's job to make sure the park's guests were happy. She walked the main pavilion with a customer satisfaction checklist on her clipboard.

Children smiling? Check.

Fast-moving lines at all rides and attractions? Check.

Dino-themed snacks, swag, and toys on sale at every shop, stand, and corner? Check, check, and check!

Suddenly, the roaring sound of an engine came from behind her, and a shadow fell over Claire. A massive truck carrying a crate with a large dinosaur had screeched to a stop.

Asset Containment Unit, thought Claire. *Oh, great. If Jurassic World's security team is here, then so is—*

Vic Hoskins jumped out of the truck. Well, he tried to. His foot caught on the door, and he landed flat on his face.

"I meant to do that!" Vic said from the ground.

Another vehicle arrived and stopped next to the truck. The door slid open and a dozen ACU guards in heavy armor also jumped out—right on top of Vic.

"Meant to do that, too," Vic's muffled voice said from under his team.

The guards helped Vic to his feet. Claire saw that the ACU had drawn the attention of many of the park guests. And not in a good way. They were looking nervously at the hungry *Carnotaurus* inside the crate.

"Uh, Vic, the whole point of theme park security is to make our guests feel *more* secure, not less," Claire said.

"Exactly!" said Vic. "That's why we've decided to hold today's practice drill in the middle of the park—so our valued customers can see just how safe they are!"

He was about to unlock the crate when Claire pushed away his hand. "Absolutely not!" she said. "Why would you even *think* about endangering our guests like that?"

"I heard that one of those Camp Cretaceous kiddos has a vlog," Vic said. "I figured that, if she shared a video of me being in charge, Vic could go viral. And I'd finally fulfill my dream of being . . . a star!"

Another shadow caught Claire's eye. Only this one was much smaller. It was a toucan flying overhead. The same toucan who had grabbed Owen's tent stake back at the campsite.

"That's weird," Claire said. "Toucans never come this close to the park. Not unless they've been—"

She watched the bird drop a tent stake, which whistled through the air as it fell. The stake landed point-first on Vic's foot, then bounced off to the side.

"Startled," Claire finished.

Vic grabbed his foot with both hands and screamed. He hopped around on his uninjured foot—only to step on the same stake with it. Vic bumped into the crate's keypad, activating the UNLOCK button.

The barred door flung wide open, and out charged the *Carnotaurus*. Some park guests pulled out their cameras, while others ran for shelter.

"Quick! Get that *Carnotaurus* back in his crate!" Claire ordered.

Vic's agents held out their shock sticks. Electricity sparked from the tips. The *Carnotaurus* shied away from the bright lights and bellowed a deafening roar. He swung his tail, tripping the ACU agents. The remaining people in the crowd stopped filming and started looking for places to hide.

The *Carnotaurus* then noticed Claire. He narrowed his eyes and began to chase her around the pavilion. She threw her clipboard at him. But the *Carnotaurus* swallowed it in one gulp and just kept on coming.

Claire gulped and thought, *Looks like I need a plan B. B as in . . .*

She saw a family that had been picnicking on the pavilion's grassy yard, until the *Carnotaurus* went berserk. They were fleeing, sandwiches in their hands, but had left behind their bright red—

"Blanket!" exclaimed Claire.

With the *Carnotaurus* closing in, Claire grabbed the picnic blanket and ran. The red fabric billowed behind her like a superhero's cape and caught the runaway dinosaur's attention. He snorted and hurtled toward her, just as Claire had hoped he would. She changed course, heading back to the ACU truck, and the *Carnotaurus* followed, his teeth about to snag the blanket. At the last second, Claire released it and jumped out of the way.

The blanket landed on the *Carnotaurus*'s face. Temporarily blinded, the dinosaur didn't see the open crate in front of him and crashed inside of it with a loud *BANG!*

Relieved, Claire went back to Vic, who was still massaging his feet. Behind him, a jumpy ACU guard crept up to the *Carnotaurus* crate. Her tranquilizer launcher shook in her hands. She was about to lock the crate when it rattled. The guard panicked and fired off a dart by accident. It whizzed off course and struck Vic right in the bottom.

The third and final scream Vic made was his loudest one yet. Claire and the ACU guards covered their ears. All of the dinosaurs within earshot groaned at Vic's yowl—especially the *Pteranodons* in the park's aviary. They flapped their wings and snapped their beaks in a frenzy, shattering the Aviary's glass walls.

The *Pteranodons* flew the coop, soaring past the *Carnotaurus* crate—which was now empty again—and Vic, who fell to the ground in a deep sleep once the tranquilizer took effect.

Claire put her head in her hands and thought, *That's one missing Carnotaurus, a flock of escaped Pteranodons, and an unconscious security officer. Just another day at Jurassic World!*

(CHAPTER 3
BAD VIBES

Back at the campsite, Owen finished pitching the last tent after several false starts. The tents were large, and there were three in total—one for the girls, one for the boys, and one for Owen and Red. The dog sniffed their tent and raised his leg.

"Red!" Owen said. "Don't. You. Dare."

Owen pulled his clicker out of his vest pocket and pressed it three times. *Click-click-click!* Red quickly lowered his leg and trotted

away. Then a young voice behind Owen said, "Hey, what's that?"

Owen turned and found Darius, followed by the other Cretaceous campers. They pointed at his clicker, and Owen said, "Oh, this? I normally use it to keep my raptors in line, not Red."

"D-d-did you say *raptors*?!" Ben stuttered.

"As in *Velociraptors*? What I'd give to race one of those!" Yaz added.

"Dude, you train raptors?" said Kenji. "That's sick!"

Owen felt flattered, then proud. He cocked an eyebrow and said, "I guess I do have a bit of a reputation as a raptor wrangler, now that you mention it. Blue, Charlie, Delta, and Echo can be deadly predators, but they all respect me."

The kids' jaws all dropped in wonder, and Owen started to think that this whole camping trip might turn out okay after all. But then Darius asked, "Can we see you control the raptors with that clicker?"

"Well, the thing is, I sort of left them back in their paddock," said Owen. "Which you guys might've noticed—*if* you'd been paying attention for the last few hours."

The kids' smiles turned into frowns. Owen felt their interest fade and quickly added, "I wanted to bring them! But Claire said no—she thought it'd be safer if we didn't mix campers and carnivorous dinos."

"Ooh, who's Claire?" asked Sammy. "Your boss?"

"No!" Owen said.

"Your *girlfriend?*" Sammy said in a singsong voice.

"NO!" Owen said, even louder. "And even if the raptors *were* with us, I don't *control* them! It's a relationship based on mutual—"

The campers groaned in disappointment. Owen tried to talk over them but was drowned out by the chorus of complaints. His eye started to twitch, and he thought, *I'm glad I didn't bring Blue and company. At least they don't have to put up with this annoying bunch!*

He held up his hands for silence and said, "Listen up, kids! This isn't exactly a walk in the theme park for me, either. But we all have a job to do. Yours is to learn survival skills, like first aid. And, yes, building tents, too! And my job is to keep all of you safe while you learn said skills. Which means we are camping far away from the local wildlife. Which means we won't see any dinosaurs this weekend."

Red had been napping nearby, but he suddenly woke up. His ears pricked, and he sniffed the air. The dog scampered over and pawed at Owen's leg for attention.

"Not now, Red," Owen said as he fought off his returning headache.

But Red insisted and bit down on Owen's pants. Then Owen and the campers felt the ground tremble beneath their feet. Ben grew nervous and asked, "I-is that an earthquake?

Costa Rica and its islands are known for their volcanic activity!"

"These vibrations remind me of my family's farm!" Sammy said. "It felt like this whenever something spooked our cattle and started a stampede!"

The kids buzzed with anxious chatter, Red barked nonstop, and the rumbling grew louder. Owen's headache and the earthquake seemed to throb in rhythm. He massaged his temples and said, "There are no stampedes on this camping trip! No earthquakes! And definitely no dinosaurs!"

That's when a herd of *Triceratops* burst out of the rainforest behind Owen. Trees toppled over and were smashed into splinters under the *Triceratops'* heavy feet.

"Uh, you were saying?" said Darius.

CHAPTER 4
UP, UGH, AND AWAY

The campers took one look at the oncoming *Triceratops* herd, freaked out, and ran in six different directions. Owen shook his head and said, "Red? Please help."

Red barked once and chased after the kids. The brave dog avoided the *Triceratops,* who had split into smaller packs. He reached Ben and prodded the boy with his snout. This made Ben veer to the left, in Darius's direction. Red then prodded Darius so that both he and Ben now ran alongside Brooklynn. Like a shepherd gathering his sheep, Red next nudged Kenji into their flock. Yaz was the farthest away, but Red quickly caught up with her, too. He guided the kids behind a large boulder, which shielded them.

Owen stood on top of a different boulder to avoid the *Triceratops*. Even from this far away, he could see that his dog had done a fine job of saving all five kids. But Owen's relief turned to dread when he remembered there were *six* campers. He scanned his surroundings and said, "Where's the chatterbox?"

"Over here!" called Sammy.

She had run in the opposite direction of the other campers, and two *Triceratops* now

cornered her. These dinosaurs were young, but the horns on their heads were still sharp.

Owen leapt off his boulder. He ran past one adult *Triceratops,* slid between the legs of another, then jumped over the tail of a third, only to almost crash into a fourth. When he came to a stop, he found himself next to Sammy and the young *Triceratops.*

"Wow, that sure was impressive, Owen!" said Sammy. "Can I call you Owen? How

about Camp Counselor Grady? Though Dave and Roxie just let us call them Dave and Roxie, so—"

"If we get out of this, you can call me whatever you want!" said Owen.

The *Triceratops* tykes charged, and Owen sprang forward, tackling Sammy. They both fell to the ground and rolled clear—just as the two *Triceratops* crashed headfirst into each other, dazing themselves.

"Whoa! Thanks, Captain Kookypants!" Sammy said to a confused Owen. "You said if we got out of this, I could call you whatever I want!"

As the young dinosaurs shook off their dizziness, Owen and Sammy met up with Red and the other campers. The reunited kids all hugged, and Owen petted Red.

"I guess we got to see some dinosaurs!" said Brooklynn.

They looked back at their campsite. The panicked animals had trampled all over the tents Owen had built, making his eye twitch again. Darius watched the herd and said, "Something must've scared them. This isn't normal behavior for *Triceratops*."

"They have thick skin, huge crowns, and triple-horns on their heads," said Yaz. "What could possibly scare *them*?"

A deep roar answered her question. The *Carnotaurus* bashed through the jungle and out into the flattened campsite.

"Toro!" Darius and Kenji whispered at the same time, their eyes widening.

The boys had narrowly survived a run-in with the dinosaur not too long ago. They

had named the *Carnotaurus* Toro, due to the bull-like horns on its head.

"That guy should be locked up at Jurassic World," said Owen. "Something must've gone wrong with the ACU. I gotta check in with Claire!"

Owen patted his vest for his cell as Ben asked, "Who's Claire again?"

"Captain Kookypants's *girlfriend*," Sammy said in her singsong voice.

"Not my girlfriend!" Owen yelled. "And that's not my name!"

He checked his pockets but couldn't find his phone. Owen felt his heart sink as he looked back at the campsite—or what was left of it. The last place he'd seen his cell was inside one of those tents. Of course, that was before those *Triceratops* tap-danced all over them. And now that Toro had arrived, an all-out dino-derby was taking place on top of the trashed tents. Owen swallowed and said, "Time for a new survival skill—tree climbing!"

"But I want to watch the dinos!" moaned Darius.

"My audience would love ground-level video of the action!" said Brooklynn.

"And *I'd* love someone to climb the tree for me," said Kenji.

"Is that poison ivy on it?" asked Ben.

"I'd rather exercise my abs—arms were *yesterday*'s workout," said Yaz.

"I'm up for climbing a tree, Captain!" said Sammy. "Do you know if there are any sloths up there, 'cause sloths are so cute, I just adore them, and did you know sloths are superslow, and I once read that a sloth's fur gets all slimy 'cause—"

Owen was so desperate to make them stop talking, he clicked his clicker. *CLICK-CLICK-CLICK-CLICK-CLICK-CLICK!* But Toro spotted the campers, hissed, and rushed past the *Triceratops* toward them.

"Go, go, go!" Owen cried.

Red nipped at the kids' rears, spurring them up the nearest ceiba tree. Yasmina led the way, followed by Darius, Kenji,

Brooklynn, Ben, and Sammy. Owen lifted Red on top of his shoulders and climbed after them. But Toro rammed his head into the trunk, shaking the tree. Everyone managed to hold on—except Yasmina. The jolt knocked her loose, and the others cried, "Yaz!"

She fell past Darius and Kenji, only to athletically twist her body in midair and catch a branch by Brooklynn. The sudden stop bruised Yaz, but at least it kept her from landing between Toro's teeth. The *Carnotaurus* roared in dismay, then went back to chasing *Triceratops*.

"Dude, I think Toro remembers us!" Kenji shouted to Darius.

"And just where do you know this Toro from?" Owen called from below.

But before either boy could explain,
two *Pteranodons*—who had escaped from
the Aviary—broke away from their flock
and swooped down. The flying dinosaurs
snatched Darius and Kenji in their talons
and dragged them skyward!

CHAPTER 5
OUT OF THE FRYING PAN . . .

"Darius! Kenji!" cried the remaining four campers.

Brooklynn pointed her cell at the two *Pteranodons* as they rejoined their flock. Her zoom lens gave a close-up of Darius's and Kenji's scared faces.

A moment later, the *Pteranodons* deposited the boys on a high, rocky cliff. The flock then landed in a ring around them, sizing up the pair of campers with their hungry, reptilian eyes. Darius got to his feet and asked Kenji, "Are you all right?"

"Not really," Kenji answered. "Why'd they shout *your* name before *mine*?"

The *Pteranodons* squawked as Kenji and Darius hugged in fear.

Owen, Red, and the others watched this all happen on Brooklynn's cell as if it were a TV show. Below them, Toro and the *Triceratops* continued to thrash across the campsite.

"There has to be a way to help Darius and Kenji!" said Sammy.

"Yeah," Brooklynn agreed. "But first we have to get past fifty yards of jungle, a rampaging *Carnotaurus,* and a topsy-turvy *Triceratops* herd!"

"No biggie," said Yaz, to lighten the mood. "Who wants to race?"

It didn't work. The four kids looked terrified, and Owen felt he should comfort them. But what could he say? It's not like they'd listened to anything else he had told them. Owen rested his clicker on a branch and patted the teens on their backs. It was awkward.

"There, there," Owen said. "We'll figure something out."

While Owen focused on the kids, something stirred in the leaves behind him. It slowly opened its mouth, slowly stuck out its long tongue, and slowly wrapped that tongue around Owen's clicker. Red finally noticed and barked. Owen turned just in time to see his clicker get swallowed by . . .

"A sloth!" Sammy shouted. "And he's so much cuter close up!"

The sloth hung upside down with its long arms, which had three extra-long fingernails on each hand. Green slime matted its fur, and its wide-set eyes gave the sloth a dopey expression.

"Hey, give that back!" Owen hollered.

The sloth closed its eyes and smiled. But that just made Owen angrier. He reached into the sloth's mouth. After a few seconds of feeling around inside, Owen pulled out his clicker. Thick saliva coated it.

"Gross!" Owen yelled, wiping his hand on Ben's shirt. Ben almost fainted.

Owen tried to use his clicker, but no sound came. Sloth spit had gummed up the device. Owen said, "That's just great! And without my cell, there's no way to call for help."

"You can use my phone!" Brooklynn said.

"I don't know Claire's phone number off the top of my head," said Owen, shaking his head. "It's saved as a contact on my cell."

Brooklynn said, "Well, I could use my cell to dial yours. If it rings, we can find it, and then you can call Claire—assuming you remember *your* phone number."

"Of course I do," Owen said. "I think."

* * *

Over on the cliff, Darius and Kenji were fending off the *Pteranodons* with some sticks they had found. The flock crept closer but stopped short when they heard . . . a song. And not just any song—a catchy song. Darius lowered his stick and said, "Huh? I love that jam!"

* * *

As the melee between Toro and the *Triceratops* led the dinosaurs away from the campsite, Brooklynn dialed Owen's number again. His cracked and scratched cell lit up in the debris below them, and the catchy ringtone played once more. Owen gave the kids a sheepish grin as they snuck down the tree.

"What?" he said, while picking up his cell. "It's got a good beat!"

Apparently, Toro liked the beat, too. The dinosaur returned to the campsite and ran headlong at Owen. There wasn't enough time to call Claire. But there *was* enough time to see her phone number on the screen and memorize it.

Owen then hurled his phone like a grenade. It bonked Toro on the head, startling him. As Owen hid behind a boulder with the others, the *Carnotaurus* sniffed at his cell. The phone vibrated with a missed-call notification. Toro swatted it away with his claw, then bounded after the cell, until both were out of sight.

"Not quite what we planned, but we'll work with it," Owen whispered.

With the *Carnotaurus* now gone, the *Triceratops* reappeared at the ruins of the campsite. Owen didn't need to be an animal behaviorist to see that they were still agitated from their clash with Toro. He tried to think of how to get around them, saying, "The only thing left in our way is that herd—"

"On it," Yaz said as she sprinted away.

"Wait!" Owen whisper-shouted after her. But she was already gone.

Yaz put two fingers in her mouth and whistled—*THWEET!*—which gained the *Triceratops'* attention. The horn-headed dinosaurs bleated in surprise and stomped after her. Owen looked at the other kids,

weighing what to do. *Stop Yaz being trampled, or help the other kids?*

There really wasn't much choice. Owen thought fast. "Right," he said, "you four stay here—I'll keep her from getting turned into Yaz-berry jelly!"

He ran after Yasmina, careful to avoid the galloping *Triceratops*. But after a few seconds, Owen slowed and doubled over with a cramp in his side.

"Help is—*gasp!*—on the—*wheeze!*—way, Yaz!" a winded Owen said.

Yaz led the herd away from the campsite. She leapt over, under, and between countless tree roots as if they were track-and-field hurdles. But the *Triceratops* weren't as graceful. Their feet tangled in the roots, and they had to use their horns to free themselves.

* * *

Meanwhile, Brooklynn grew impatient as she, Sammy, Ben, and Red waited behind the boulder. Poking out her head, Brooklynn saw the cliff where the *Pteranodons* had landed, and she said, "It doesn't look good. We can't just hide and do nothing! We've got to help Darius and Kenji!"

"But Mr. Grady said to stay here," Ben reminded her.

Red bit down on Brooklynn's jacket to force her to stay put, then heard a faint chittering sound. Several *Compsognathus* appeared at the sides and top of the boulder. A moment later there were dozens of them—enough to make *everyone* reconsider Owen's orders.

"Ya know, I'm suddenly with Brooklynn!" Sammy said. "Let's get the guys!"

Even Red had to agree. He and the three kids abandoned the boulder, which was now overrun with *Compsognathus*, and hightailed it to the camp wreckage. They retrieved two trampled tents, then made their way to the cliff. Fortunately, there were enough ledges for them to climb. At the top, they saw the *Pteranodons* snap at Darius's and Kenji's sticks with their beaks, keeping the boys boxed in between them. Red barked, spooking the dinosaurs. They took to the air and circled overhead like vultures.

Sammy held up the tents and said, "Everyone, unfold and twist!"

She, Brooklynn, and Darius grabbed the ends of one tent. Kenji, Ben, and Red (who used his teeth) grabbed the ends of the other. Ben looked over the cliff's edge and said, "I have mentioned my fear of heights before, haven't I?"

"For once, I agree with Ben!" added Kenji. "That's, like, a fifty-foot drop! I'd rather take my chances up here!"

Suddenly, one of the *Pteranodons* swooped down, narrowly missing Kenji's perfect hair. He ducked, swallowed, and said, "On second thought . . ."

The kids twisted the tents into two ropes, then tied them together to form one longer rope. Red bit down on one end, anchoring it, and the kids climbed down. His paws skidded on loose gravel as the campers went, but Red never let go. A few feet below the cliff, the kids found an outcrop they could stand on. Brooklynn held out her arms and said, "Red! Jump!"

The dog released the rope and leapt down toward them. Brooklynn caught him, and Red licked her cheek in appreciation. Darius looked to the side and saw a set of sturdy-looking rocks jutting from the side of the cliff.

"I think we can use those as steps!" he said.

Darius and the others bundled up the tent "ropes" just in case they might need them again and hopped carefully from one rocky stair to the next. The *Pteranodons* spiraled after them, but it was Ben's fear of heights that made him shriek in terror. His earsplitting cries kept the *Pteranodons* at bay, allowing the campers and Red to safely descend the natural steps all the way to the ground.

Yaz raced over to them, while Owen lagged behind her, limping and panting. He held up a finger and caught his breath, then said, "I thought I said 'stay here'!"

Owen then saw the tent-rope coiled in Ben's hands, adding, "And I thought *you* were allergic to synthetic fabric!"

Ben looked down at his rash-free fingers and said, "Huh. I guess I *could*'ve helped you build those tents after all, Mr. Grady."

Owen slapped his forehead, then said, "All in favor of returning to the Camp Cretaceous tree house early, say aye."

"Aye!" said all six campers.

CHAPTER 6
. . . AND INTO THE FIRE

Claire's phone rang, the screen displaying an unfamiliar number.

"Claire Dearing," she answered. "Who's this?"

"Your favorite raptor wrangler," Owen said over the line, joking. "I'm calling from Brooklynn's phone. Um, say, Claire, you wouldn't happen to be missing one big *Carnotaurus* and/or a flock of hungry *Pteranodons*, would you?"

Claire's jaw dropped, and she said, "How could you possibly know about—"

KSSH! KSSH!

Loud static interrupted their call before the line went dead.

"Owen? Can you hear me?" Claire asked. "Are you there?"

* * *

Far across Isla Nublar, Owen checked Brooklynn's phone. The signal icon showed zero bars, and the battery had dropped to fifty percent.

Jurassic World can clone dinosaurs, but they can't build enough cell towers?! Owen thought.

He returned the useless cell to Brooklynn, who marched behind him, followed by Darius, Kenji, Yaz, Ben, and Sammy. Red kept them in a single-file line, and the kids took turns carrying the two rolled-up tent-ropes. As their troop reached the top of a hill, they could see the tree house in the distance.

"Just another brisk thirty-minute hike, and you'll be back to Wi-Fi, air-conditioning, and microwave burritos," said Owen.

CROAK!

The sound came from a nearby bush. Owen halted in midstep. The campers also froze in place, but it was too late.

CROAK! CROAK!

That had come from a different bush. Owen looked around and knew that his group had been hemmed in. Something in the bushes rustled around them, and out stepped a pair of *Baryonyxes* sporting two snaggletoothed sneers.

Owen whispered, "When I say so, I want you kids to r—"

"Run—got it!" Yaz said in a hurry.

And just like that, she was off. The other kids bolted after her. Owen chased after them with Red, shouting, "I was gonna say 'release the tents'! Not *run*! Running is the exact thing *not* to do!"

The *Baryonyxes* surged forward. Their claws helped them zigzag through the tall buffalo grass. But Ben wasn't quite so nimble. He tripped and tumbled downhill, coming to a stop at the bottom—in front of a giant pit.

"Help!" Ben yelled.

The pit appeared to be twenty feet wide and at least twice as deep. Ben crawled away from the brink, but the soil gave way beneath his sneakers, sending him over the edge. His hands flailed and found a thick root. He held on for dear life, until his fingers started to slip. As if that weren't bad enough, the two *Baryonyxes* peered over at him, flashing their many, many fangs.

"Hang on!" hollered Owen.

"Yeah, I wasn't planning on letting go!" Ben yelled back from inside the pit.

The *Baryonyxes* turned away from Ben to face Owen and Red. The dinosaurs croaked at each other. It sounded like an argument, and Owen thought, *They're probably wondering who's the tastier snack—me, Red, or Ben!*

As the leering *Baryonyxes* focused on Owen, he motioned for Red to help Ben. The dog clamped down on Ben's collar, pulled him out of the pit, and dragged him back up the hill. Red and Ben joined the other campers at the top, where Darius shouted, "*Baryonyxes* are piscivorous—they eat fish! So, um, try using a fish!"

"Thanks!" Owen yelled while dodging claws. "Too bad I don't have a spare fish on me! Must've left it in my other vest!"

"You don't have to sound so sarcastic!" Brooklynn yelled back.

The *Baryonyxes* backed Owen against the side of the hill. He felt his vest pockets for something—anything—that could possibly save him. But all Owen found was his clicker. He shook it next to his ear and heard liquid sloshing. Owen aimed the button end at the *Baryonyxes* and said, "I think there's something stuck inside. Could you please take a look?"

Then Owen clicked his clicker. A small stream of smelly sloth spit squirted the closest *Baryonyx* in the eye. The surprised dinosaur recoiled in disgust, colliding with the second one. With the two *Baryonyxes* busy hissing and sniping at each other, Owen used the distraction to race uphill and shout, "*Now it's okay to run!*"

He and Red led the kids away from the pit and into a new stretch of rainforest, one that Owen didn't recognize. The vines grew denser here, and the light dimmer. But the sounds grew louder. Everyone heard the gurgle of rushing water. Sammy pointed ahead and said, "A river!"

"It's okay!" Owen said as they stopped at the riverbank. "I've jumped into a river to escape dinosaurs before!"

Yaz stepped forward to take a closer look. She picked up a pebble and dropped it into the water. It instantly disappeared beneath the flurry of fast-moving currents.

"Looks rough," she said.

"And cold," Kenji added.

"And deep," Sammy said.

"And piranha infested," finished Ben.

In the end, the *Baryonyxes* made up the kids' minds for them. At least, their roaring did. Owen heard the ravenous noises the dinosaurs were making as they rustled through the jungle and remembered that *Baryonyxes* were strong swimmers. If he and the kids were to escape them, they'd need as much of a head start as possible. So Owen pushed the campers into the water, one by one. They each landed with a splash, followed

by Red and Owen, who also hopped into the
river before the *Baryonyxes* arrived.

The current whisked all of them—and
two rolled-up tents—away faster than the
big *Baryonyxes* could swim. Unfortunately,
the river also whisked them away from the
Camp Cretaceous tree house.

CHAPTER 7
THAT SINKING FEELING

As it turned out, the river wasn't as chilly or as piranha infested as the campers had first thought. But before they got too comfortable, Owen felt the current pick up speed. The river took a sharp turn, and Owen's worst fears were confirmed.

"Rapids!" he shouted.

The kids swam against the flow in a panic but only succeeded in tiring themselves. Big black rocks jutted out of the water downstream. Owen figured they would smash the kids to pieces if he didn't act fast. He called to the kids over the raging river, saying, "The tents! Unroll them now!"

Kenji and Yaz did as they were told. The fabric unfolded into two triangles, giving everyone something to hold on to in the surf. Owen spat out water and said, "These have built-in air mattresses! Find the rip cords!"

Darius felt around the nearest tent and found a cord that ended in a plastic toggle. Sammy found the exact same thing on the other tent. They both pulled their cords, and the mattresses inside each of the two tents instantly inflated, making them float like balloons.

"These tents are just as hard to break as they are to build!" said Owen. "All aboard!"

He, Darius, Ben, and Brooklynn climbed onto one raft, while Yaz, Sammy, Kenji, and Red got onto the other. And just in time, too. They pinballed off the rocks. But Owen knew a few more hits like that might puncture the air mattresses.

"We're not out of the woods—er, waves— yet!" he said.

Owen pulled out three metal tubes from his raft. He screwed the pieces into each other, forming a long crossbar. Normally, this would have supported the tent's roof. Owen showed it to the teens on the other raft and said, "Now find one of these!"

Yaz assembled the tubes with Sammy's and Kenji's help. Following Owen's lead, they used the two poles to push themselves off the next rocks. The plan worked, and

they navigated the rest of the rapids without capsizing. As they went downriver, the current finally slowed.

"Yes!" the kids all cheered at once.

The roar of the rapids faded in the distance, only to be replaced by a new disturbing sound—a loud buzz that was growing even louder. Large shadows flitted overhead. Darius squinted and said, "Oh no . . . are those *Pteranodons* back?!"

The flock flew lower, and Owen realized that it wasn't actually a flock. It was a swarm of enormous mosquitoes. They seemed almost prehistoric, and the volume of their sinister drone doubled as they dive-bombed the rafts.

Owen used his pole to swat away first one big bug, then another. Yaz did the same. But there were too many for the two of them to handle.

Ben pulled a can of bug spray from his fanny pack and said, "Mom said this would come in handy!"

He sprayed the repellent, which clung around their raft like a cloud. Owen then lobbed the can over to the second raft and said, "Fetch!"

Red caught it like a frisbee, and Sammy sprayed a similar cloud, making the mosquitoes buzz off.

After that, nobody said anything for a while. This silence remained even after Owen had pulled the rafts out onto a remote riverbank. The sun had long since set, and the kids found it hard to see. They took stock of their few supplies. With the exception of Brooklynn's cell—which still had no signal— all of their other belongings were either waterlogged, damaged, or dinosaur food.

"Some survival training," Brooklynn muttered. "How's anyone supposed to survive *this*?"

Owen overheard her but didn't have much of an answer. Claire had entrusted him to teach these six kids. Yet here they all were, in some uncharted area of Isla Nublar—lost, wet, and cold. Owen couldn't help but blame himself. He, Red, and the kids were still alive though, and that was something. All Owen had to do now was keep them that way.

He gathered dry sticks and moss into a pile. Owen then pulled two flint stones from one of his pockets. They were a little damp but still usable, so he struck the flints together. It took a few tries, but they soon gave off sparks. Those sparks landed on the sticks and moss, which caught fire. Owen gazed into the flames for a moment.

Without a word, the kids and Red warmed themselves around the campfire. Owen took the rip cords from the rafts and tied them into a single line. He fastened one end of the line to the tip of his tent pole. Then Owen tied the other end to a paper clip that he had bent into a hook.

"Boom," said Owen. "Instant fishing rod."

He cast his line and hoped for a bite. He felt his luck change as something tugged on the hook.

"No way!" Owen said. "That was fast! I think I got one!"

The kids perked up, grinning and rubbing their bellies as he reeled in his catch. And when Owen finally pulled his hook out of the river, they saw a glistening fish on the end of it—big enough to feed seven starving humans and one hungry hound. Owen grinned at his accomplishment and said, "Looks like seafood is on the menu after—"

The line snapped. The fish flopped back into the water. And the kids' smiles disappeared. Owen tossed his fishing rod onto the riverbank in frustration as the teens began to gripe again, making Red howl. Owen's headache returned, and his empty stomach rumbled. Raising his voice above the others, he said, "Bedtime! Everyone find a branch and try to catch some shut-eye."

Sammy, Yaz, Ben, and Brooklynn climbed up a tall tree. But Kenji and Darius still needed a little convincing.

"Uh, are you sure that's the best idea?" Darius said.

"The last time we went up a tree, I almost became lunch," Kenji added.

Owen shrugged and said, "Suit yourselves. Red?"

He patted his shoulders, and Red hopped on top of them. Together, they climbed the tree and found a branch big enough for two. Back on the jungle floor, Darius and Kenji heard a faraway roar. They hurried up the tree after the others.

As the moon shone behind the clouds, each member of this little expedition felt too worried to sleep. Darius tossed and turned on his branch. He had loved dinosaurs ever since since his dad had introduced him to them. But after today, Darius wondered if he might be in over his head at Camp Cretaceous.

The next branch over, a blue glow lit Brooklynn's face. She whispered into her cell, saying, "What up, Brooklanders? Between this island's spotty Wi-Fi and dangerous dinos, I don't know if this will upload. Um, ever. Either way, please enjoy this video of the hilarious Red dragging his rear end on Owen's tent. And don't forget to subscribe and comment below. G'night."

As Brooklynn shut off her phone, she saw that it had less than twenty-five percent of battery life left. Kenji was glad that Brooklynn had finished vlogging. He needed to concentrate as he rubbed ceiba tree sap into his scalp. Kenji thought he might have discovered a terrific new hair product out here in the wild. At least, that was what he *tried* to think about. Because if Kenji didn't think about his hair, then he would have to think about how useless he felt on this island.

On the branch above Kenji, Yaz used the burnt end of a stick from the campfire to draw on the bark. She sketched a perfect copy of the Camp Cretaceous tree house and was struck by a surprising homesickness. Yaz erased the drawing with her sleeve before anyone else could see it.

Across from her, Ben shivered. But not from the cold. He shivered with fright. Every sound Ben heard seemed amplified in his head. A stick snapped nearby. Or maybe it was a crackle from the fire. Or could it have been a razor-sharp claw scraping up the tree? Whatever it was, Ben didn't want to find out.

Sammy heard Ben's teeth chattering from her branch. She wanted to say something to soothe him. But much to her own surprise, Sammy didn't feel like talking.

On the lowest branch of the tree, Owen used Red as a pillow. The dog was having a dream—or a nightmare, from the sounds of it. Probably involving a *Carnotaurus.* Or *Pteranodon.* Or *Baryonyx.* Or all three. Owen petted Red's fur and saw a shooting star above them.

So Owen wished for a way to return Red and the kids to Jurassic World, alive and unharmed. Somehow . . .

CHAPTER 8
DIAL *D* FOR DINOSAUR!

Early the next morning, Claire found Owen's phone in a muddy *Carnotaurus* footprint. She had told the ACU team to track Owen's cell the moment she had lost her connection to Brooklynn's phone. But Owen's device was malfunctioning after getting stomped and kicked around the island, so locating it had taken longer than expected. By the time the phone's weak signal brought the caravan of ACU vehicles to this patch of jungle, Owen,

Red, and the campers were nowhere to be found.

However, Vic's squad *did* find the *Pteranodon* flock in the area—just as Owen had hinted in his call with Claire—and netted the flying dinosaurs as they slept in their new nest.

"Like catching fish in a barrel," said a smug Vic. "Only these fish fly. And they aren't fish."

The ACU team loaded the last of the *Pteranodons* into their trucks. Once the cage

doors were locked, Vic said, "Good going, gang! The ACU saves the day yet again! Now, let's party!"

A truck driver cranked up the radio. The sudden noise startled the same jittery ACU guard who had accidentally fired her tranquilizer at Vic the day before. She shot another dart right into Vic's bottom.

"Seriously?!" Vic cried.

He was about to yell at the jumpy guard when suddenly a loopy smile appeared on his face. Then he collapsed face-first into the muddy footprint, sound asleep.

Claire rolled her eyes. She knew that Owen, Red, and the kids were still somewhere out there, and needed help. Claire dialed Brooklynn's number again, hoping her call might go through this time. A moment later, someone picked up. But instead of a friendly hello, Claire heard a long scream, followed by a loud *THUD!*

"Is it a dinosaur attack?!" gasped Claire.

"No, we're fine," Brooklynn said into her cell. "Well, mostly. My ringtone startled Owen, and he kinda fell out of our tree."

"Ouch," said Claire.

Brooklynn shimmied down the trunk and handed her cell to Owen, who rubbed his bruised back. The other kids and Red climbed down from their branches, yawning and stretching.

"We're going to pinpoint Brooklynn's cell, then send a chopper to your location," Claire told Owen. "All you need to do is stay on the line a little long—"

Owen and the kids never heard the end of her sentence. The battery icon on the phone showed zero percent before the screen abruptly went dark. Brooklynn dropped to her knees, devastated, and yelled, "Noooooooooooo!"

The others helped her up. After Brooklynn had recovered a bit, she said, "Maybe I shouldn't have taken those last four videos of Red snoring."

Rain started to fall. Ben reached into his fanny pack and pulled out a clear plastic poncho. After he put it on, the five other campers and Red all tried to climb under the poncho as if it were an umbrella. It was a tight fit, and the kids and dog all got smooshed together. But at least they were dry. Owen wrung the rain out of his shirt and said, "If we're lucky, Claire and the ACU team may have locked on to our signal before the battery died."

Darius tugged Owen's vest and said, "What happens if we *aren't* lucky?" He pointed to the river, where an old fallen tree on their side connected one bank to the other. Toro was now crossing that tree and roaring.

The kids skedaddled, followed by Owen and Red and, of course, the *Carnotaurus.* Toro must've had a good night's sleep, because he ran at top speed. But Owen and the kids moved much slower than yesterday. Their stomachs were empty, and their legs were tired. There was no way they'd be able to outrun Toro now . . . not that they'd had much of a chance anyway.

CROAK! CROAK!

Owen and the kids froze. The *Baryonyxes* blocked their path. They crept closer, just as Toro approached behind the group. Owen and the kids were surrounded. Yaz asked, "What do we do now?!"

"I'm open to suggestions," said Owen.

"Too bad our rafts don't have wheels," Sammy said with a nervous laugh.

"That'd never work," said Kenji. "The jungle's too muddy from this rain. We'd have to make skids, like my dad's company uses. But for that, we'd need lumber. And something to tie it all together. And most importantly, a power source to drive it. Like I said, it'd never work."

Owen felt like a light bulb had turned on in his head. Perhaps it was the hunger or the lack of sleep—or the three dinosaurs breathing down his neck—but Owen reached into Ben's fanny pack and said, "You don't mind, do you?"

He pulled out the can of bug spray and threw it at Toro. The *Carnotaurus* bit into the can, which immediately exploded in a huge cloud. Neither Toro nor the two *Baryonyxes* could see through it. Using the haze as a cover, Owen and Red led the kids back to the river rafts.

"You wanted survival training?" Owen asked them. "This is it! You guys work in

teams to build Kenji's contraption. Kenji will tell you what to do."

"Me?!" Kenji cried. "What about you and Red?"

Owen pulled the poncho off Ben, ripped it in half, and said, "Okay, team! Pay attention! Here's the plan. . . ."

* * *

Back in the rainforest, Toro and the two *Baryonyxes* coughed because of the bug spray. But the fumes that had temporarily blinded them were now evaporating. And without any humans around to feed upon, the smaller dinosaurs shrank away from Toro, lest they become the *Carnotaurus*'s next meal.

The *Baryonyxes* scurried into a thicket of bushes, then sniffed the air. Detecting a scent, they grew alert and prowled forward a few paces into a clearing. They saw Owen Grady standing there, waiting for them.

"Remember me?" he said.

The *Baryonyxes* screeched, and Owen fled toward the river with the two dinosaurs in hot pursuit. He grinned and said, "Those campers better be ready. . . ."

* * *

At the side of the river, Brooklynn hauled two flat planks of driftwood from the water. She set them in front of Darius, who used his raptor-tooth necklace to cut up one tent. Kenji then took those ribbons of fabric to tie the remaining raft to the driftwood skids. And Yaz and Sammy turned the last two strips into a matching set of wide loops as Ben and Red dragged over what appeared to be two plastic bags filled with water.

Everyone took a step back and admired their work. Darius, Brooklynn, Ben, Sammy, and Yaz all high-fived. They had built Jurassic World's first land raft!

Kenji said, "But we still need a power source."

"Taken care of!" Owen yelled.

He ran up to them with the *Baryonyxes* tailing him like heat-seeking missiles. Owen signaled to Sammy and Yaz and said, "Now!"

The girls twirled the fabric loops over their heads like a pair of lassos and released them at just the right time. The loops cinched tightly around the *Baryonyxes'* necks, and Sammy said, "Atta girl, Yaz! This is just like bein' back on my family farm!"

"Thanks for teaching me rope handling, cowhand!" Yaz said back.

The *Baryonyxes* bucked and hissed, putting up quite a struggle against the lassos. Brooklynn and the boys helped Sammy and Yaz, while Owen knotted the other ends of the lassos to the front of the sled.

Enraged by their capture, the *Baryonyxes* charged the humans. But when they did, the lines around their necks, now secured to the sled, dragged the campers' vehicle behind them. It followed the *Baryonyxes* step for step, confusing and upsetting them. To shift the dinosaurs' attention in the direction of the tree house, Yaz and Kenji raised the two raft poles from the night before. Only now the tips of the poles held those water-filled plastic bags made from the halves of Ben's poncho. Inside each of these makeshift aquariums swam a big fish.

Red shook his drenched fur. He'd gotten soaked when he dove into the river to catch the fish.

Owen looked back at the *Baryonyxes*. The sight of their favorite food made them laser focused on the suspended fishbowls. Owen motioned for everyone to get on the sled as the dinosaurs' eyes followed the bobbing bags of fish that Yaz and Kenji held out in front of them.

But before anyone could get too settled, Toro plowed out of the rainforest. The *Carnotaurus* roared, and Owen cried, "Next stop: Camp Cretaceous!"

Yaz and Kenji stood on the front of the sled and lowered the poles, dangling the water bags before the *Baryonxes*. The dinosaurs lunged and ran after the fish—which were

always just out of their reach. This made
the *Baryonyxes* move at incredible speed, even
while towing the land raft behind them.
Owen and the kids looked at each other in
surprise and held on tight. Their plan was
working!

The jungle became a blur as the dino-
powered vehicle spirited them toward the
tree house—and away from Toro.

CHAPTER 9
THIS IS THE PITS

"Keep your arms and legs inside the vehicle at all times!" Owen said, sounding like the announcement from Jurassic World's rides. *Too bad the vehicle doesn't have seat belts!* he thought. *Or seats!*

The land raft bounced over the wild terrain. It swerved around boulders and dodged low-hanging tree limbs. Owen, Red, and the six campers had to duck on several occasions.

But Yaz and Kenji held their poles steady. The fish swam in the water bags just in front of the *Baryonyxes'* snouts, and the dinosaurs showed no signs of slowing down.

Neither did Toro, who still trailed doggedly after them. While the *Baryonyx*-led sled avoided obstacles, Toro simply bashed through them. His horned head sent those same tree limbs and boulders flying. They landed like cannonballs around the land raft and covered everyone in mud.

"My hair!" Kenji cried.

He handed his pole to Darius, then pulled a compact mirror from his pocket to check his hairdo. In the reflection, Kenji saw Toro gaining on them. Darius struggled with the pole and yelled, "Objects in mirrors are closer than they appear!"

Toro bit off the back of the sled. The kids screamed and scrambled to the front. Owen saw an enormous *Stegosaurus* skeleton ahead and said, "Lean right!"

All six campers sat on the right side. Their combined weight made the sled tilt in that direction just as the *Baryonyxes* turned. The land raft narrowly avoided the skeleton—but lost its left skid in the process.

Toro didn't fare as well. The angry *Carnotaurus* plowed right into the bones. They tripped him up, but he was soon recovered and chasing his prey once again. The sled still rocketed through the jungle. But with one skid missing, the road now felt much bumpier. More pieces of their vehicle snapped off.

"We're not gonna make it to the tree house, are we?" said Sammy.

"Not like this," Owen agreed. "We need to stop that *Carnotaurus*."

"What about the pit?" asked Ben. "That's big enough to hold him, right?"

Another roar boomed as Toro caught up with them. Sunlight glinted off the

Carnotaurus's teeth, and the kids could smell rotten meat on the dinosaur's breath.

"Pee-yew!" said Sammy. "Does anyone have a ginormous mint?"

"Nope," said Owen. "But we *do* have a blindfold!"

He yanked on one of the tattered flaps of tent that Toro had shredded, which hung on by a thread. It took some effort—these tents were durable, after all—but Owen tore it free and let it go. The flap fluttered in the air before landing on Toro's face, covering his eyes. His arms were too tiny to reach it to get it off, but Toro kept charging after the land raft.

Owen, Red, and the campers felt the ground below them start to rise. The *Baryonyxes* had led them all the way back to the grassy hill. Yaz and Darius kept the fish in front of them, and Owen kept a tight grip on the ropes. They climbed higher and higher. Behind them, Toro blindly chased and clawed.

Once they reached the top, Owen yelled, "Hard right!"

Yaz and Darius swung the fish poles, the other campers shifted onto the right half of the sled again, and the *Baryonyxes* turned.

But Toro did not. He ran straight off the hill. Gravity pulled the *Carnotaurus* down into the pit. Toro landed at the bottom and bellowed in outrage.

The land raft fell apart for good at the base of the hill. Fortunately, Owen, Red, and the campers were protected from any serious injury by the inflated mattress. But

the crash also snapped the lassos. Now freed,
the *Baryonyxes* had their sights on the fish—
and the campers sprawled around them.
The two dinosaurs' jaws opened wide and—
WHUP! WHUP! WHUP!

The noise made every human, dog, and dinosaur look up to the sky. A Jurassic World helicopter hovered overhead. Claire and the park's owner, Mr. Masrani, waved at Owen from the cockpit.

The *Baryonyxes* screeched at the sound of the spinning rotors. They forgot about the fish and bolted into the jungle. The coast was now clear, so the campers dumped the bait back into the river. The fish swam away faster than any fish had ever swum before.

Owen limped over to the edge of the pit and saw Toro glowering back at him. The *Carnotaurus* gave one final roar, and Owen said, "Yeah, yeah, I get cranky when I'm hungry, too."

CHAPTER 10
SEEING RED

As the chopper landed on the Jurassic World helipad, waiters in tuxedos greeted the six exhausted kids, Owen, and Red with a parade of fancy dining carts. The campers stepped out of the helicopter and made a beeline for the carts. The waiters offered them a variety of beverages. Then they brought trays full of scrambled eggs, buttered toast, fresh fruit— and phone chargers. Brooklynn jumped for joy as she plugged in her cell.

"Rolling out the VIP breakfast buffet, huh?" Owen said to Claire as they left the chopper.

"I know you were supposed to be roughing it this weekend," she replied. "But they've had it rough enough. And my job is to keep our guests happy."

The campers ignored the plates and silverware and stuffed fistfuls of food into their mouths.

"I can't tell who has worse table manners," said Claire. "These kids or the dinosaurs."

Once the platters had been licked clean by the campers and Red, Darius said, "I suppose this means our survival training is over."

"I suppose," said Owen. "Try not to look too excited."

But to Owen's amazement, the kids didn't look excited at all. In fact, they looked downright sad.

"I know we got off on the wrong foot," said Owen. "I mean, none of you could put up a single tent yesterday."

The teens lowered their heads in embarrassment.

"But that was yesterday," Owen continued. "Look at everything you've done since then."

"I guess we learned how to fish," said Yaz.

"And build fires," said Ben.

"And ropes," said Darius.

"And rafts," said Brooklynn.

"And a land raft," said Kenji. "Although it actually looked a lot like a sled."

"And we learned about the many uses of sloth spit," said Sammy.

This last comment confused Claire. But Owen looked out at the vast jungle beyond the theme park and said, "You've learned how to deal with whatever nature throws at you. That's what survival training's all about. So congratulations—you all graduate from Captain Kookypants's Survival Training Camp with degrees in creativity and improvisation!"

"Huh? Captain Kookypants?" Claire muttered, more confused than ever.

All six campers threw their arms around Owen. The sudden gesture left Owen feeling surprisingly moved.

"Stay strong, Grady," he whispered to himself.

"Did somebody mention creativity and improvisation?"

Everyone turned and saw Vic strutting onto the helipad with a cage full of *Compsognathuses*. As the little dinosaurs squeaked and climbed the bars, Vic added, "Then you're gonna love my patented dino-handling techniques! I taught Owen practically everything he knows!"

The boast made Owen and Claire trade looks of disbelief, and they sensed that this wouldn't end well. But Vic opened the cage and reached inside for a wriggling dinosaur, saying "Now, just watch as I expertly train a *Compy* to—"

Before Vic could snag the *Compsognathus,* it chomped down on his hand. He screamed and dropped the cage, which landed on his bruised feet. This made Vic cry out

again—and that cry only grew louder as the *Compsognathuses* escaped the open cage and skittered all over him.

"I can't wait to put this on my vlog!" Brooklynn said over Vic's squealing.

As Owen calmly and carefully plucked the *Compsognathuses* off Vic, Brooklynn aimed her now charged cell at the spectacle, pressed the button to record, and . . .

"Oops," said Brooklynn, checking the device. "This hasn't recorded anything new since last night. I must've taken too much footage of Red."

"Huh?" Vic said softly from the helipad floor.

Brooklynn tapped the UPLOAD button on her screen, and several videos of Red appeared on Brooklynn's vlog. The campers

watched one of Red dragging his rear end over Owen's tent and said, "Awww!"

Red looked away innocently as Owen glared at him. Ben then pointed at Brooklynn's screen and said, "The likes on your vlog are going through the roof!"

"By the thousands—tens of thousands!" said Sammy.

"It's trending across all platforms!" said Kenji.

"This must be a new record, Brooklynn!" said Darius.

"I couldn't have done it without Red," she said.

As Brooklynn and the other kids petted Red, Vic hitched up his belt and walked away, moping.

Claire watched him go and said, "Well, looks like it's back to the day job for him!"

And for me, Owen thought as the campers laughed and watched more Red videos. *After babysitting six teenagers, I want something simpler and a lot more peaceful—like training a pack of deadly raptors!*

CARNOTAURUS

A large carnivorous dinosaur with small forelimbs, long hind limbs, and a massive head on a muscular neck. The distinctive horns above the eyes are this predator's unique feature.

I saw one named Toro up close, and I was never worried about his horns. I was more worried about his teeth. Trust me, they were BIG!

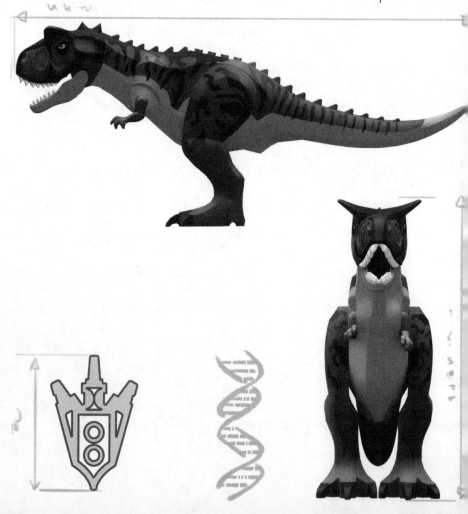

SIZE: ■■■■■

Explains why Toro's footsteps were so loud when he chased us!

STRENGTH: ■■■■■

SPEED: ■■■■□

Not so fast! We ran away from him . . . okay, I guess we were lucky!

ATTACK: ■■■■■

INTELLIGENCE: ■■■▨▨

True. Toro's not much of a thinker!

CONTAINMENT:

Extremely dangerous species. Needs to be kept only in a closed compound secured with high-voltage fence. Requires nonstop supervision.

> I suggest even more supervision. Seriously! I could feel Toro's foul breath on my neck when he wasn't supervised enough!

CHARACTERISTICS:

Rams an opponent with its small horns. The analyses conducted by John Hammond and his team suggest that *Carnotauruses* use very quick but not very strong bites.

> Totally agree. I saw Toro attack, and I'd rather not see it again!

OPERATIONAL COMMENTS:

A high level of aggression. Further observation recommended to determine whether the asset can be displayed as one of the park's attractions.

> "A high level of aggression . . ." Really? Toro's bar on the aggression chart would be as tall as Toro himself, if you ask me!